# The New FOLKLORE

Lyrical Tales for Dreamers & Thinkers

# The New FOLKLORE

*Lyrical Tales for Dreamers & Thinkers*

Text by
**Teague Alexy**

Illustrated by
**Sally Flanagan**
**Chris Monroe**
**Jeredt Runions**
**Nicholas David**
**Clare Grill**
**Christine DeRosa**

NORTH STAR PRESS OF ST. CLOUD, INC.
St. Cloud, Minnesota

Kathleen Flanagan, Anne Rasset, Corinne Dwyer—editing

Kathleen Flanagan, Joshua Priestly, Curtis Weinrich, Angelo DeRosa, Vicki Joan Keck—consulting

Corinne Dwyer, Curtis Weinrich, Anne Rasset, Rob Litsenberger—design and layout

"How Lefty Stepanovich Turned Water Into Wine" was previously published by Ivy Arts Copy & Print of Minneapolis, Minnesota, in 2014.

ISBN: 978-1-68201-005-1

Printed in the United States of America.

Published by
North Star Press of St. Cloud, Inc.
P.O. Box 451
St. Cloud, MN 56302

www.northstarpress.com

*To the Flanagan Family*

# Table of Contents

The New
FOLKLORE

# The Wisdom of King Joe Colli

Illustrated by Sally Flanagan

I am here to tell a tale
And help the wise and otherwise understand
That the wisest man ever to walk on land
Was ol' King Joe Colli.

Don Von Braughan, from a distant land,

Had squeezed many a wise man's neck with his strong and mighty hands.

He marched on Colli's kingdom, intent to make it his own,

And found only a note on King Joe Colli's throne.

*Gold is for the color of my kingdom,*

*Green for the color of the land.*

*Red is for the blood of my people.*

*May it never spill while entrusted in these, my humble hands.*

*Sincerely, King Joe Colli*

So Don Von Braughan made himself at home,

Resting his feet on the king's table, while sitting on the king's throne.

He filled the king's cups with the king's fine wines,

And had the royal marking placed on his forehead, which was common in those times.

He mused, "Maybe King Colli is as wise as they have said,

For had he not fled, I would surely have his head."

There was not a thing the townspeople could do

When Von Braughan proclaimed the new colors of the kingdom: Gray and Blue.

The new flag flew,

With its ho-hum hue,

High above the imposter and his crown.

The only glimpse of light or hope

Was in the eyes of those who spoke

Of a new entertainer in town.

Von Braughan decided to see for himself, and found a juggler on the street
Wearing a fool's headdress and a dimwit's beard that grew halfway to his feet.
He was juggling bright balls of red, gold and green,
Tosses and tricks, the likes of which Von Braughan had never seen.

"I am an entertainer, and we need entertainers in this world
As we need doctors and teachers, the laughter of little girls.
We need things to think about, things to make us smile
And lighten our burdens for just a little while.
If I make your day a bit brighter than it's been,
Pay the favor forward, drop a nickel in my tin.
If your belly and pockets are empty, take my performance as gift.
Tell me your troubles, my friends, and share in my tips."

The juggler collected a modest dime. Von Braughan cheered, "Good show!
But what is the meaning of the old kingdom's colors?" he demanded to know.

"Pardon me, Your Highness, for not throwing the gray and the blue.

These are not meant as colors of any man-made kingdom, old or new.

I need bright balls against these black and deep skies.

One cannot catch what one cannot see, no matter how one tries."

Sensing himself a victim of the juggler's wit, Von Braughan felt a hint of shame.

He had no interest in this vagabond's simple mind games.

Von Braughan disliked jesters, jokers and jugheads from way back.

The knowing juggler smiled and returned his needle to the haystack.

"Yours are a wise king's feet
To leave the palace and walk the street.
Minding the concerns of the people, Your Majesty,
Writes a king's story
One of triumph and glory.
Ignoring the people spells tragedy."

"Since your cowardly King Colli has fled to a faraway land,
And my ploy to purge his palace proceeding precisely as planned,
With good men guarding the palace and my best men chasing Colli down,
I nobly proclaim this juggler to perform on behalf of the crown."

"With all due respect, Your Majesty, I prefer a crowd of common man
To performing for the fortunate, at royalty's command.
I am a true artist. Only compromise I fear.
My act has no strings attached. I need no puppeteer."

Von Braughan had killed for less disrespectful behavior,
But he sensed an oppurtunity to win the people's favor.
"You will not have to change your act or the color of your juggling balls,
And are as welcome to perform in the streets as within my castle walls."

The strongest storm of the season accompanied the juggler as he approached the gates

With a gift of white poppy flowers for his host. The guard announced, "The king awaits!"

Boastful, brazen and loose-lipped Von Braughan said, "It's not that I care for your entertaining.
It's that, while you perform, the people stop complaining.
Always crying for me to fill their bellies up."
The juggler rubbed a familiar thumb along the side of the royal cup.

"If I may propose a toast:
Here's to keeping our enemies closer than the friends that we keep close."

Von Braughan added mindlessly, "May nothing exceed like excess,"
And eagerly threw back his head to have another drink with his guest.

With the speed of an ace magician or sorcerer at his best,
The juggler yielded a sword and stuck it through Don Von Braughan's breast.
The juggler's headdress fell slowly. Von Braughan's eyes filled with dread,
Discovering two in the room with the royal marking upon their head.

By gosh!
By golly!
By all things wise!
If that wasn't ol' King Joe Colli in a juggler's disguise.

As Von Braughan lay still on this, his final night,
Dark clouds cleared, the stars again were bright.
The words of King Joe Colli echoed through the streets.
The kingdom's true colors danced in the moonlight.

"Gold is for the theft of my kingdom.
Green for the neglect of the land.
Red is for your wicked blood.
May it be the last to stain these, my humble hands."

# Old Lady Truth

## Illustration by Chris Monroe

Hezekiah was a man whose days had been well spent.

He had it all, but all he had did not make him content.

"I need to find truth," he said, and left all he had of worth.

Over mountains, valleys, deserts and seas he went on his noble search.

For a time it seemed his journey would be of little use,

Until one day a man told him where he could at last find truth.

"Yes, Old Lady Truth. She lives high above the town, just below the skies."

Hezekiah's search for truth had yielded lies, lies, lies.

He climbed the mountain anyway with all his strength and might,

And crawled into a cave to get some shelter for the night.

Sure enough, there was the old woman, just as the townsman had said,

With ragged hair, warts on her face and not a single tooth in her head.

Of course he had his doubts but when he heard her voice so lyrical and pure,

He knew he had found truth—he was absolutely sure!


He stayed a year and a day with her, learning all she had to teach.

He stood at the mouth of the cave and made ready to leave.

"My Lady Truth, you have taught me so well, I'd like to do something for you."

What the old lady could possibly want, Hezekiah hadn't a clue.

She raised an ancient finger, and, with a smile difficult to see,

She said, "Tell the people I am young and I am beautiful, whenever you speak of me."

# The New Tune of Elijah Swoon

**Illustrated by Jeredt Runions**

Elijah Swoon
Sang a tune
On a Saturday afternoon,
Wearing his Sunday best.
On his way down
To the town
To show everyone around
How he could pull his heart out of his own chest.

He hardly noticed the man with an old tin can and a sign that read
GOOD ADVICE, TENFOLD YOUR MONEY'S WORTH.

The man had shoes few feet could use, tapping and whistling "I
Mean You." Elijah walked on by.

Elijah put himself up on display, but the people had doubts if the heart in his hand had come from within his own chest.

By hook, by crook, everywhere you look, honest covers on crooked books. So many hearts sold for so much less.

"There's no gloss or shine on this heart of mine! No pine tar! No turpentine!" Elijah hung his head and pointed his shoes toward home.

"I thought by showing this heart of mine, maybe some would take the time for a good long look at their own."

Elijah Swoon, dressed in gloom, dropped a dime in the man's tin can. The man gently wiped the spit from his lip.

"In time you'll find peace of mind with those who drag their hearts behind and others who follow theirs off the side of a cliff.

This world is made of you and me and him and her and on and on, but you can't force love on anyone.

Keep your heart inside your ribs. Protect it as the jewel it is. Reveal it through each breath of your lungs."

Elijah grinned, so benevolent, turned his heel and off he went, barefoot, whistling "I Mean You."

If you're in town and need advice,
Spare change is a small price
For the man with an old tin can
And Sunday shoes.

# Three Little Fish

**Illustrated by Nicholas David**

One big fish swimming in the sea.

He is hungry. Big fish always seem to be.

Big fish always seem to be.

Three little fish swimming in the sea.
The big fish is hungry enough to eat all three.
Hungry enough to eat all three.

A funny thing happened that bright, fine
day.

The big fish ate one little fish, the other
two got away.

Why did he let them go? The big fish knew
better.

The two little fish that swam away, they
were swimming together.

The New
FOLKLORE

# How Lefty Stepanovich Turned Water Into Wine

## Illustrated by Sally Flanagan

All the good folks in the town of Mealdathyme

Decided to see who could be the first to turn water into wine.

The winner was sure to become famous, noble and rich.

So everyone set to task. Well, everyone except Lefty Stepanovich.

"Mine is the machine," exclaimed Mr. Borkinszankersneer,

"That will be the first to quench our thirst with fortune and good cheer."

So, with plans in his hands and a pep in his step,

He worked forty days and forty nights, with hardly time for rest.

The whole town gathered 'round with excitement in their eyes.

Folks came from as far as Kanzabar and as wide as Fort Tellilize.

"I will now provide proof and put to practice my pleasure-producing prototype."

The people were pleased as it pitter-pattered, popped, purred and pumped water
    through the pipes

And poured a port-like potion so red a man declared, "It must be fabulous!"

But upon a closer look, it was merely water mixed with rust.

Before the crowd could even sigh, arose the voice of Mr. Klumpherness.

"I've just assembled the final piece of a model I got at the Mess-4-Less.

Come all ye people, come drink from my still."

But his wine tasted like turpentine with a hint of chlorophyll.

So the two men came together to put a new plan intact.

Inventing a new invention might bring the nobility they lacked.

For fortune they'd little need, both were men of great wealth.

They plotted and schemed over vintner's Reserve pulled from the top shelf.

And looking out at Lefty sitting in the shade of his trees,

They quipped, "Lefty must expect his wine to come blowing in on a breeze."

They poked fun at Lefty as *vino* soaked the night.

"The reason they call him Lefty is because his logic isn't right."

Laugh, and oh, did they laugh, stomping their feet on the floor.

When, alas, they heard a knock and opened up the door.

"I am merely a wanderer. I hate to trouble you, my good man,
But my thirst outweighs my pride, so in front of you I stand.
I can only offer my grace, if you might be kind enough
To grant some water from your well and fill my empty cup."

"Well, maybe you can't read," sneered Mr. Borkinszankersneer,
"But this sign says NO TRESPASSING. You're not welcome 'round here.
The only pity you'll get from me, you old bum,
Is I'll be walking real slow to go and get my gun."

Many moons passed over the town of Mealdathyme,

With no man the wiser of how to turn water into wine.

Mr. Borkinszankersneer worked away in cap and overalls,

While Mr. Klumpherness searched the world's greatest shopping malls.

Gallant efforts made by many, for want of fame and admiration,

Usually exploded or were kicked to pieces in frustration.


'Til one day the old wanderer reappeared, this time a spring in his step.

He walked past Mrs. Borkinszankersneer and Mrs. Klumpherness.

A wooden wagon he pulled behind him, bigger than anything on the road.

He must have been much stronger than he looked, to carry such a load.

He greeted the ladies with a smile and a tip of his hat.

They recognized him as the man on their doorstep a good while back.


"Please join us for tea, and tell us what brings you back this way.

We are curious as kittens as to the contents of your wagon, we must say."

"On behalf of your conscience, ladies, you need not compensate.

I hold no grudge toward you nor your husbands. It's not worth the extra weight.

I have just a small token in return for the greatest gift in the universe—

A simple glass of water when I was dying of thirst.

This wagon is full of the world's finest wine, if truth be told.

A lifetime supply for your good neighbor, Lefty—even if he lives to be three
   hundred years old."


The old man grinned, in spite of himself, before letting out a laugh.

He pulled the wagon to a roll and said, "Farewell," as the ladies stood aghast.

"Who would've thought? Of all the people in Mealdathyme,

It was Lefty Stepanovich who discovered how to turn water into wine."

# Teufelo's Tongue

### Illustration by Clare Grill

They cut off Teufelo's tongue for claiming to be an angel. Now he's judged a thief. Gonna
  hang from the gallows pole.
Maiden Molly McAbee says, "I love that boy from the bottom of my soul.
As long as he holds my hand I will never grow old."

Mr. McAbee, the merchant, spoke, "I know not who stole the diamonds you speak of,
But I know who holds the heart of my dearest daughter, be him a thief, an angel, or just a
  fool in love.
Release him in the name of my family and the good Lord above."

"Boy, you shall die a cruel death if you return to Seraphree as long as the grass shall grow.
It hurts me to say, Miss McAbee, you are no longer welcome as long as the north winds blow.
We will cut off his arm for punishment and leave them go."

One can only guess what was going through the mind of the folks in the town of Seraphree
When Teufelo picked up his arm, put it back on his shoulder, and around the waist of
  Maiden Molly McAbee.
They went walking toward the mountains with a mouth full of diamonds where his tongue
  used to be.

# Old Rickety Bridge

Illustrated by Christine DeRosa

Thaddeus was walking on that old, rickety bridge.

That old, rickety bridge?

That old, rickety bridge.

When destiny in the form

Of Miss Mona Clayborn

Came slowly walking on by.

Crazy, drunken Uncle Fate, look what ya done did.

Look what ya done did?

Look what ya done and did.

Now, Thaddy walks around with his head up in the sky.

Oh me. Oh me. Oh my.

Thaddy was always such a sweet and innocent kid.
Sweet and innocent kid?
Such a sweet, sweet kid.
Was gonna go a long way,
Bring back a fortune some day.
Never was any type of romantic guy.

But he swears he saw sunshine behind her eyelids.

Behind her eyelids?

Behind her eyelids.

And looked up to see the moon on high.

Oh me. Oh me. Oh my.

## Notes

### "The Wisdom of King Joe Colli"

– High elf rune *Urithair*—means "destruction" and "conquest." Used for Don Von Braughan's battle flag as he approaches the castle.

– This symbol means "harmony." Used on the front of the castle's balcony.

– High elf rune *Ceyl*—means "law," "order," "justice" and "passion." Used as the "royal mark."

– *Fleur de lis*—the translation is "flower of the lily" and signifies perfection, light and life. Used on the castle and on the royal crown Von Braughan is wearing.

– The juggler is quoting William Shakespeare within the line, "I need bright balls against these black and deep skies." This is a reference to *Macbeth*: "Stars, hide your fires, let not light see my black and deep desires."

– The white poppy flower is known as a symbol of peace, especially in times of war.

– Colli (CAWL - lee)

– Don Von Braughan (Don Von Brawn)

### "Old Lady Truth"

– Based on the classic folktale "Old Lady In the Cave."

### "The New Tune of Elijah Swoon"

– "I Mean You" is an American be-bop era jazz composition written by Thelonious Monk and Coleman Hawkins.

### "How Lefty Stepanovich Turned Water Into Wine"

- Mealdathyme (Me - ALL - dah - time)
- Stepanovich (Step - ANNE - oh - vitch)
- Borkinszankersneer (BOR - kins - ZAYNK - er - sneer)
- Kanzabar (KANZ - ih - bar)
- Tellilize (TELL - lie - lies)
- Klumpherness (CLUMP - fur - ness)

### "Teufelo's Tongue"

- Teufelo (TOO - fell - oh)
- Seraphree (SAIR - a - free)

### "Old Rickety Bridge"

- The name "Thaddeus" means "heart."

- The recurring symbol of the red-winged blackbird is in memory of the author's Irish grandmother, Nora Flanagan, who often said she would return as a red-winged blackbird.

## About the Author

Teague Alexy is an award-winning singer, songwriter and musician living in Minnesota. He has released three albums: *The New Folklore, This Dance* and *A Gentleman Named Actionslave*. In 2005, Teague and his brother Ian formed the American roots music band Hobo Nephews of Uncle Frank. Hobo Nephews tour the United States from coast to coast and have released five albums: *Hobo Nephews of Uncle Frank, Sing!, Traveling Show, Number One Contender* and *American Shuffle*. For more information, please visit www.teaguealexy.com.

## About the Illustrators

Sally Flanagan is an illustrator and photographer. She trained at the Fleisher Art Memorial in Philadelphia, holds a degree from the Art Institute of Philadelphia and received her Bachelor of Arts from the University of Pennsylvania. Sally currently resides on the South Jersey Coast.

Chris Monroe is an author, illustrator and cartoonist living in Duluth, Minnesota. She is a graduate of the Minneapolis College of Art and Design. Chris is the author and illustrator of award-winning picture books *Sneaky Sheep, Cookie The Walker, Bug On A Bike* and the Monkey With A Tool Belt series. Her books have been translated into five languages.She is also the creator of the comic strip *Violet Days*, celebrating its nineteenth year in print.

Jeredt Runions is a painter, illustrator and craft beer brewer living in Wisconsin. He has a Bachelor of Fine Arts in studio art and geography from the University of Wisconsin – Superior.

Nicholas David is a singer, songwriter, vocalist, musician, voice-over actor and illustrator living in St. Paul, Minnesota. Nicholas had memorable performances on the 2012 season of NBC's *The Voice* and his 2013 EP *Say Goodbye* reached #2 on the iTunes album chart. As leader of The Feelin Band, Nicholas plays piano and sings alongside Teague Alexy on the album version of *The New Folklore*. Nicholas also reads the part of Mr. Borkinszankersneer on the audio version of "How Lefty Stepanovich Turned Water Into Wine." For more information, please visit www.thefeelin.com.

Clare Grill is a painter living in Queens, New York. She received her Bachelor of Arts from the University of St. Thomas in Saint Paul, Minnesota, a Master of Fine Arts from the Pratt Institute in Brooklyn and attended the Skowhegan School of Painting and Sculpture. Clare's solo exhibitions in Los Angeles and New York have been featured in *The Los Angeles Times* and *The New York Times*, who raved, "Ms. Grill's control of pictorial space is precise yet magical." For more information, please visit www.claregrill.com.

Christine DeRosa is an illustrator and mother of three living on the South Jersey Coast.

# Audio Versions

**"The Wisdom of King Joe Colli"**
Teague Alexy & The Feelin Band. Check teaguealexy.com for more details.

**"Old Lady Truth"**
Available on Teague Alexy & The Feelin Band's album *The New Folklore*.

**"The New Tune of Elijah Swoon"**
Check teaguealexy.com for more details.

**"Three Little Fish"**
Available on Teague Alexy & The Feelin Band's album *The New Folklore*.

**"How Lefty Stepanovich Turned Water Into Wine"**
Digital single by Teague Alexy & The Feelin Band is now available.

**"Teufelo's Tongue"**
Available on Teague Alexy & The Feelin Band's album *The New Folklore*.

**"Old Rickety Bridge"**
Check teaguealexy.com for more details.

The original album version of *The New Folklore* by Teague Alexy & The Feelin Band was released in 2006 and is available as a digital download. Check teaguealexy.com for more details.